THE BOY ON THE BEACH

THE BOY

For Margaret K. McElderry, with love and friendship from Niki

First published in Great Britain in 1999 by Bloomsbury Publishing Plc
36 Soho Square, London, W1D 3QY
This paperback edition first published in 2005

First published in America in 1999
by Margaret McElderry books, Simon & Schuster Children's Division, New York

Text and illustrations copyright © Niki Daly 1999
The moral right of the author/illustrator has been asserted

Printed in Belgium by Proost

5 7 9 10 8 6 4

All papers used by Bloomsbury Publishing are natural,
recyclable products made from wood grown
in well-managed forests. The manufacturing
processes conform to the environmental
regulations of the country of origin.

ON THE BEACH

Story and Pictures by

Niki Daly

BLOOMSBURY
CHILDREN'S
BOOKS

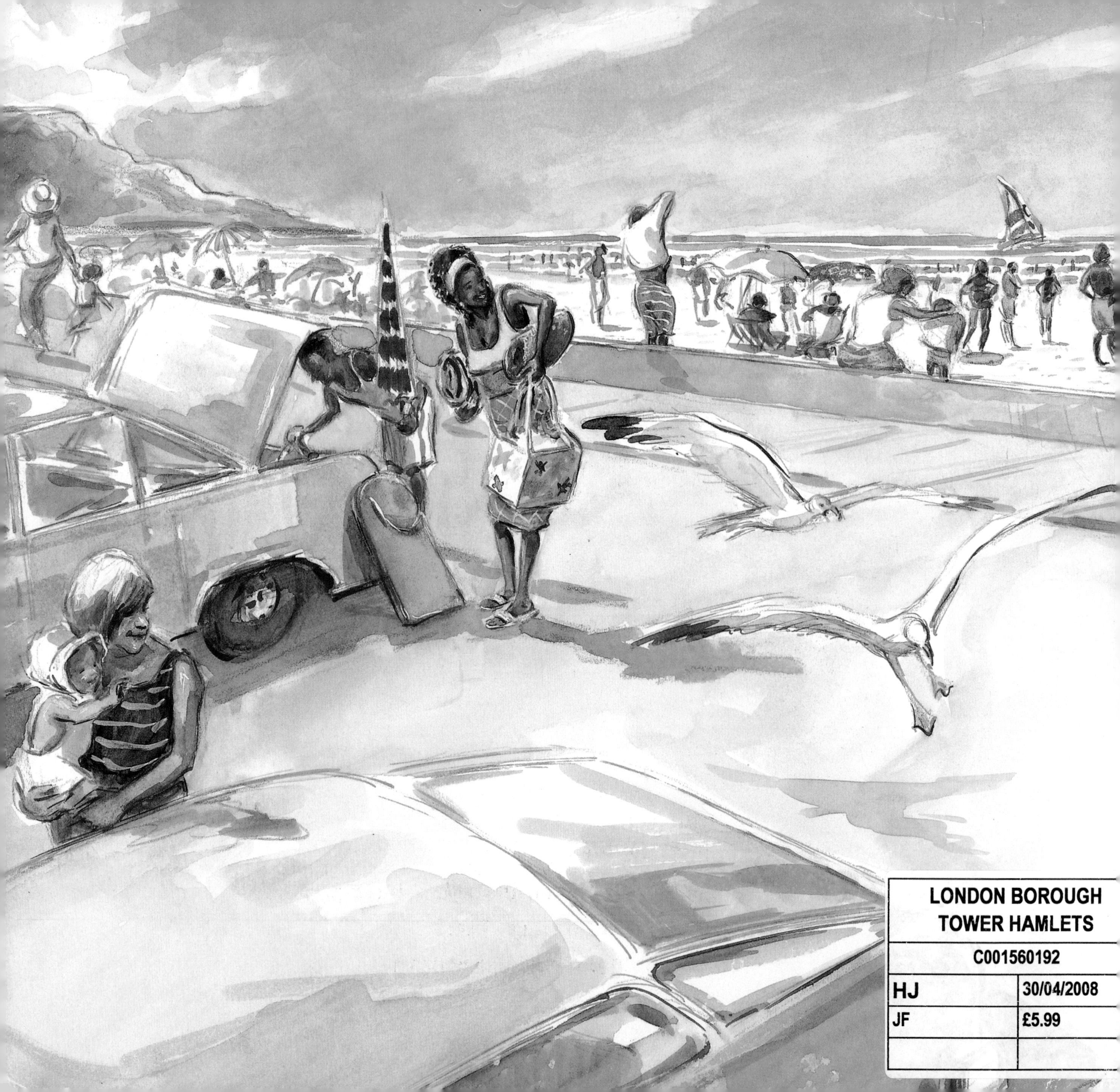

It's hot, hot, hot—
hot as sun-melted tar in the beach car park
"Stay close, or you'll get lost!"
calls Mum to the boy on the beach.

Between bright umbrellas and tropical towels
they find their spot.

Sandy toes . . .

sun-cream nose . . .

camera smile–*click!*

And off he goes . . .

castle-bashing . . .

rock-pool splashing . . .

surf crashing—

wet, wet, wet . . .

. . . wetting Mum, who likes to take it slow,
and Dad, who's waiting for the BIG ONE.
"Come, take my hand!" says Mum.
But the boy on the beach stands only ankle-deep
because there's just *too* much water out there.
"Come on, grab hands and you'll be all right
when the big one comes," says Dad.

SPLASH!

"Now, that wasn't too bad," says Mum.
"One more time! And I'll buy you a king-size Twister
with sprinkles on top," says Dad.
But the boy on the beach says,
"NOOOO!" And off he goes . . .

leaping . . .

bumping . . .

kangaroo jumping—spraying sand wherever he goes.

SLOW DOWN!

See him zip through the crowd like a high-speed boat—
past surfers and sailboards and lazy sunbathers.
Zigzag around a smelly, shaking, shaggy dog—
but there's no time to play a wild seaweedy game.

Look there! Perched high on a dune
stands the lifeguard's lookout—
just the place on the beach for a boy to go.

And below, in a hollow, lies an old boat, waiting . . .

. . .waiting for a captain who isn't afraid of
sharks and storms and BIG ONES
that can knock a man right overboard.

Help! Help! Help!

All around, sand dunes rise like monster waves,
and the boy on the beach feels lost and alone.

"Mummy! . . . Daaadddy!"

Here comes the lifeguard—
as cool as a coke
and copper-tanned.
"What's up, kid?"
"I want my mum and dad,"
cries the boy on the beach.

Piggyback, over the dunes, along the crowded beach the boy goes—
all the way to Lost and Found, where his mum and dad are
waiting for him.

"There was a terrible storm. I fell out of my boat and saw a shark. The waves were EVEN BIGGER than the BIG ONE!"
"I'm glad you're safe," says Mum happily. "Now, how about that king-size Twister with sprinkles on top?" says Dad.
"Cool," says the boy on the beach, "*and* one for my lifeguard."

"My name's Bruce, but my friends call me Speedo.
What's your name, kid?" asks Speedo.
But the boy on the beach just can't stop licking.
"Tell him," says Mum. "Go on," says Dad.

A king-size Twister with sprinkles on top is *far* too yummy for a boy to talk. So, with pointed toe in the soft wet sand, he begins to write . . .

Joe.